Sirens

I live for beauty – it's my life.

Si•ren (sī'rən), noun.
A seductively
beautiful or
charming woman,
especially
one who
beguiles men.

marco glaviano

SIRENS

A CALLAWAY BOOK

WARNER ⓦ TREASURES®

PUBLISHED BY WARNER BOOKS

A TIME WARNER COMPANY

To ADRIANA, BARBARA, ALESSIA
AND ADRIANNA GLAVIANO
AND TO MY NUMBER ONE SHEILA.

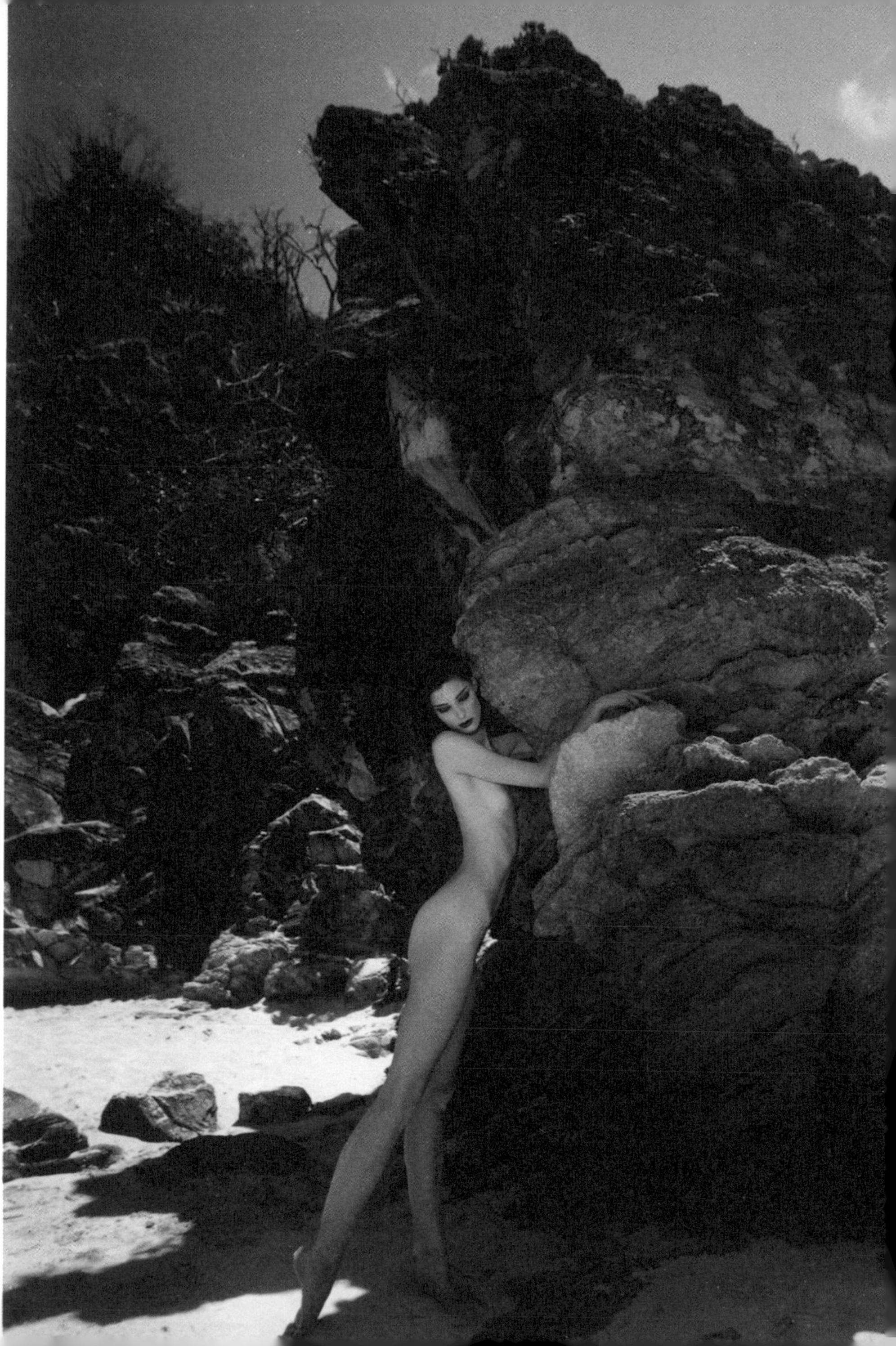

Anneliese Seubert, St. Barth, 1995

Cindy
Crawford
Cabo
San
Lucas
1991

Cindy Crawford has a beauty you cannot disguise. She is not a model, she's an enterprise. Some people become like that through hard work and determination, but I suspect Cindy knew what she wanted the day she left the crib. She's different from anybody else I've ever seen in this business. She's professional and precise in everything: never even one minute late and so organized– Cindy knows exactly what she's doing, what she's wearing, and why. She also knows what she doesn't want to do. Nobody has ever pushed her around – no agencies, no men, no photographers, and she's totally dedicated when it comes to work. We've had our ups and downs, of course, but basically it's been a great relationship.

Cindy Crawford, Bahamas, 1992

Cindy Crawford, Cabo San Lucas, 1991

Cindy Crawford, St. Barth, 1989

Cindy: Marco, it's too *Vogue.*

Marco: You're right. But think of yourself as a pop icon. You're the pin-up revisited.

Cindy Crawford, Bahamas, 1990

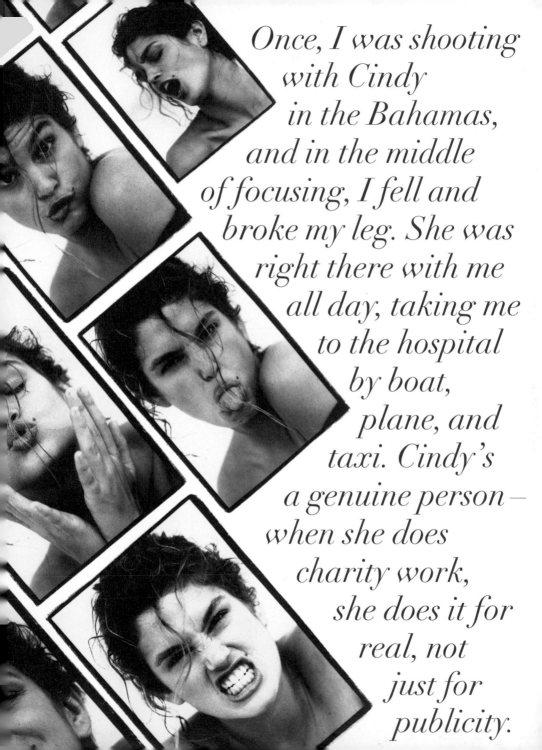

Once, I was shooting with Cindy in the Bahamas, and in the middle of focusing, I fell and broke my leg. She was right there with me all day, taking me to the hospital by boat, plane, and taxi. Cindy's a genuine person – when she does charity work, she does it for real, not just for publicity.

Cindy Crawford. St. Barth. 1992

When we started working together on the first calendar, we fought a lot. I think Cindy wanted to be in control and show me who was boss. One day we had a little argument over a background and she remarked, "And don't you think I'm going to take a picture with a parrot on my shoulder." She was referring to a picture in the previous year's calendar of Paulina with a parrot on her shoulder. I replied, "That's such a beautiful picture, you're never going to be able to do one as beautiful as that!" Then she started yelling, and **I said, "You know, you're not Miss Congeniality,** are you?" I stomped off the set to my hotel room; she stormed off to hers. The next day we made up and finished the shoot. The last night on location I was sitting at the restaurant where we all hung out. Suddenly the lights went down, and Cindy came out of the back in front of all these tourists, wearing a bathing suit and a ribbon across her chest that said "Miss Congeniality" and a fake parrot perched on her shoulder. She took me completely by surprise.

Cindy Crawford, St. Barth, 1989

Cindy

Crawford

Bahamas

1992

Cindy Crawford, Cabo San Lucas, 1991

EVA HERZIGOVA, ST. BARTH, 1993

EVA HERZIGOVA, ST. BARTH, 1993

Eva Herzigova, St. Barth, 1993

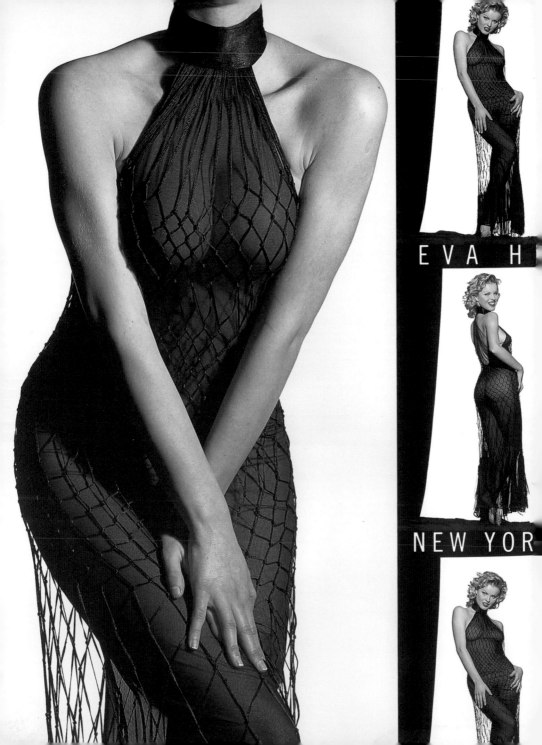

EVA H

NEW YOR

GOVA

TY 1994

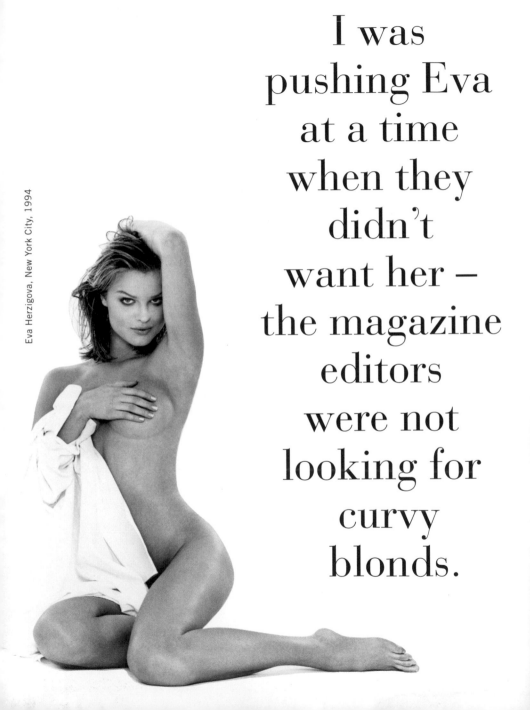

Eva Herzigova, New York City, 1994

I was pushing Eva at a time when they didn't want her – the magazine editors were not looking for curvy blonds.

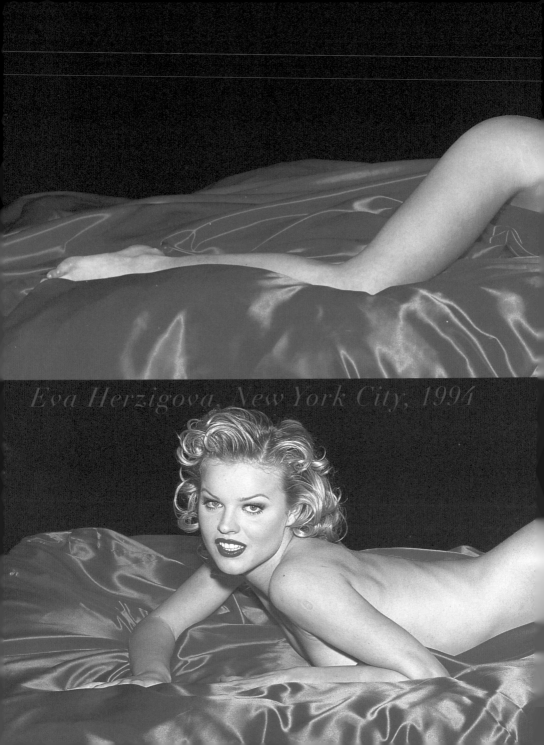

Eva Herzigova, New York City, 1994

I take beautiful pictures of men, flowers, landscapes, rocks, jazz musicians, and other things, but the public is more interested in the women I shoot. It's not the end of the world.

That's just the way it is.

Eva Herzigova, St. Barth, 1993

Eva

Herzigova

St.

Barth

1993

ANNA
FALCHI

Anna Falchi Stromboli 1995

Anna Falchi, Stromboli, 1995

I took these pictures of Anna, an Italian actress, for a calendar for an Italian magazine. They gave it away as a promotion with the Christmas issue, and it more than doubled their sales.

Everything on Stromboli is black — black sand, black rock, black everything. I love black, but after four days at this place I was craving color! The volcano on the island is still very active — every day you can feel the earth trembling beneath your feet, and there's a constant flow of lava down one side to the ocean. It gets really nerve-racking after just a couple of days.

Anna Falchi, Stromboli, 1995

Anna Falchi, Stromboli, 1995

BEVERLY

I first met Beverly when she came to St. Barth with her mother and stayed in the same hotel where I was staying – although I was shooting with Cindy at the time. Beverly was shooting with Patrick Demarchelier. Patrick and I would have a drink at the hotel bar, while the assistants and models fought over the ball playing water polo in the pool.

Beverly Peele, St. Barth, 1992

Usually I find that I take my best photographs in leftover times after shoots for clients. I'll go on a trip to a place, do the work, and then I'll take an extra two hours or two days, whatever I have time for, to do my own thing. If it feels right, everyone wants to keep going even when they're tired.

Lisa Berkley, St. Barth, 1980

Niki Taylor

When I first met Niki I tried to talk her out of modeling, because I think there's an age for everything. I just thought she should go out and have fun with her friends first. I'm glad she didn't listen to me, but I still think enjoying youth is more important than modeling.

24   KODAK 5063 TX

24   ▷ 24A

Niki Taylor, New York City, 1991

Niki Taylor, Miami Beach, 1992

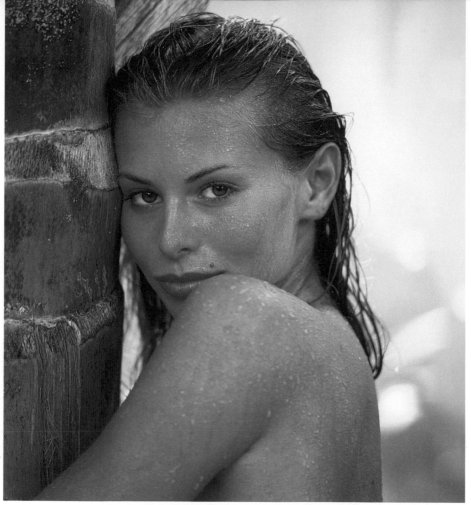

When Niki first arrived at my studio with her mother,

she moved better than anybody I'd ever seen.

I asked her where she learned to move like that, and she said, "Oh, I've been practicing in front of a mirror for years."

Niki Taylor, St. Barth, 1992

JILL GOODACRE

Haiti, 1984

When I travel I talk to the local people rather than the tourist office, so I get to know the secret places. Eventually somebody takes you to a place you're not supposed to go to — this waterfall in Haiti is considered sacred. This never ran in the magazine I was shooting it for. Some of what I consider my best pictures have never been published, I guess because they're not interesting enough at the time. It's not uncommon, though, for the same people who turned it down before to become interested later.

ST. BARTH

Mel Flagler, St. Barth, 1992

I'VE BEEN SHOOTING AN INCREDIBLE TREE ON

St.Barth

Ashley Richardson, St. Barth, 1984

for over 20 years. I've shot at least five different models posing with it – I always
go back again to try to do it a little bit better. This tree has so much character.

Ashley Richardson, St. Barth, 1984

*This is a view from that tree
on St. Barth. Over to the
left is the car we used to go
to the shoot. I tell you,*

St. Barth is one of the most beautiful corners of the world.

*It looks a little bit like Ireland
and Sardinia combined –
not Caribbean at all. There's
always wind, and the sea
is always rough. There are rocks
and no beach on this side
of the island, and the long,
dry grass moves with
the wind like the waves.*

I love this place.

*Unfortunately,
the tree
was killed
in a
hurricane
in December
1995.
I felt sad
when I
went back
and found
it laying on
the ground
dead.*

Stacey Ness, St. Barth, 1996

Stacey
Ness
St. Barth
1996

Daniela Pestova, St. Barth, 1993

My friend Edith posed for this shot. Edith is much too short to be a model, but this picture proves you don't have to be a top model to take a beautiful picture. It's the system that decided a woman has to be six feet tall.

Edith, St. Barth, 1987

Elizabeth, St. Barth, 1990

How much more beautiful can you get than Michelangelo's *David*? Why is it acceptable for naked men and women with perfect bodies to exist as art, but not in photography? People are affected by what society and culture tell them is good or bad, or right and wrong. They believe what they are told, and their opinion is colored. That makes it difficult for people to see anything for what it really is.

Adriana Sklenarikova, St. Barth, 1995

Stacey Ness, St. Barth, 1996

ELIZABETH, ST. BARTH, 1990

Elizabeth, St. Barth, 1990

Ingrid Seynhaeve, St. Barth, 1992

Ingrid Seynhaeve, St. Barth, 1992

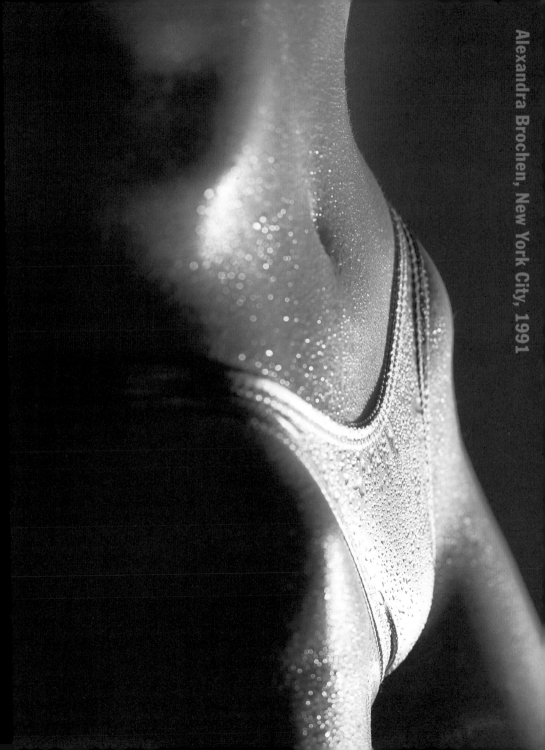

Alexandra Brochen, New York City, 1991

There's a
famous Brassai
print of a
sailor smoking
in bed.
I redid that
shot with
Lisa Berkley,
who was
my wife at
the time.

Eva Herzigova, St. Barth, 1993

Lisa Berkley, St. Barth, 1982

Eva Herzigova, St. Barth, 1993

There's something fabulous about a beautiful blond with a round figure and blue eyes.

Lisa Berkley, St. Barth, 1982

Mel Flagler, St. Barth, 1991

Claudia

Claudia Schiffer, St. Barth, 1990

When I photograph women, I usually bring out the best in them, but they are also doing it themselves. They feel confident, because they know I will take a flattering picture of them. They see in my pictures that I've made it my job to show women in their best light. That trust and confidence is what's important. They also know that I refuse to abuse the privilege of working with these gorgeous creatures by never using a photograph they don't like.

Claudia Schiffer, St. Barth, 1990

Claudia Schiffer, St. Barth, 1990

When I first met Paulina she
was positively wild, like a
kid. She wasn't crazy about
modeling and wasn't afraid
to show it. She would go
around saying, "Modeling
sucks. Modeling sucks."
This is a business where
everybody kisses ass, but
Paulina never did. She also
never went to a party she
didn't want to go to, and she
never even dated anybody
in the business. When she
had the Estée Lauder
contract, she drove them all
crazy because she allowed
herself to be seen buying
other brands of cosmetics. I
tell you, she didn't care
about her career. In spite of
all that, she had one of
the biggest modeling careers
and still does.

Paulina Porizkova, St. Barth, 1987

Paulina Porizkova, New York City, 1987

Paulina Porizkova
New York City
1987

**On the way to St. Barth for a calendar shoot, Paulina and I stopped
and they're basically not much more than a sandbar with a few**

Paulina Porizkova, Sandy Cay, 1986

...t this deserted island. There are lots of them in the Caribbean,
...alm trees. The funny thing is, they're all called Sandy Cay.

Paulina Porizkova, Anguilla, 1987

American Vogue

PAULINA DOES:

American Glamour

"Dumb model pretends to be intellectual"

Sophisticated European

Cosmopolitan

Paulina Faces, New York City, 1991

Jack Nicholson

Seventeen

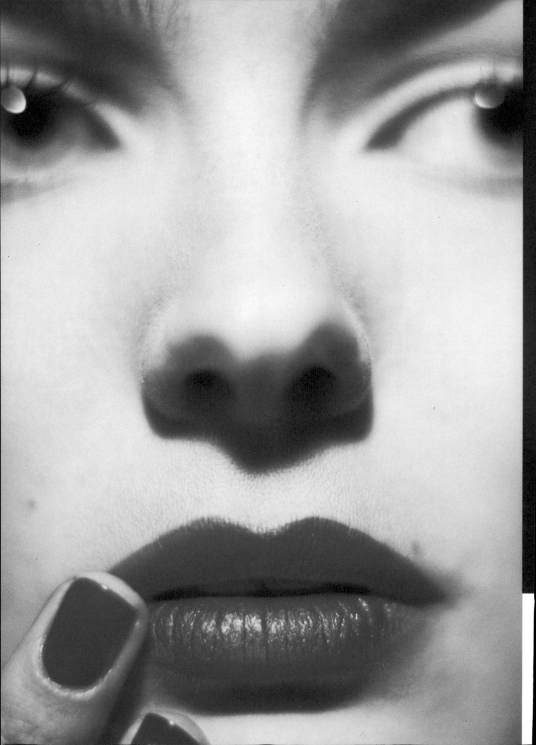

Paulina
is
perfection

down to

the part.

She's so

beautiful,

I'd call her

a freak
of nature.

Paulina
Porizkova
Anguilla
1988

Paulina Porizkova, Moustique, 1987

Paulina Porizkova, St. Barth, 1989

I was the photographer at Paulina's wedding. Here she is one hour before she married Ric Ocasek — she was a nervous wreck and smoking like a fiend! She and Ric had rented four houses on St. Barth for the wedding, and all 23 guests stayed for a week. All the magazines and newspapers wanted their wedding pictures, but I wouldn't sell them out of respect for Ric and Paulina.

This is one of the best photographs I ever took of Paulina. It's a very difficult picture, because she had to tilt her head back and up, and then whip it around and come out of it with such a great expression on her face.

It's something only Paulina could do

Paulina

Porizkova

New York City

1986

PAULINA PORIZKOVA, RENE SIMONSEN, CAROL ALT, NANCY DE WEIR, JOAN SEVERANCE, NEW YORK CITY, 1983

These were the supermodels of the '80s. After everything was set up I had to wait for them — the five top models in the world — to get into position. They were actually fighting to be in front! They were elbowing each other and jostling around for position, and then in came Paulina, who just put her foot down and her back to the rest of them and refused to be a part of all the pushing. It never ran in *Harper's Bazaar*, because I left the outer poles and the backdrop visible. I was trying something new, keeping the poles in, but they didn't like it.

We couldn't get all the girls together at the same time, so this was taken in two shoots and pasted together later. I shot Niki and Eva one day, then Amber, Beverly, and Daniela the next.

Niki Taylor

Eva Herzigova

Amber Smith

Beverly Peele

Daniela Pestova

St. Barth, 1992

behind closed doors

Cynthia Antonio, Paris, 1993

Aimee McKenney, Milan, 1995

For a lingerie shoot I decided to imitate

art of hyperrealist painter John Kacere.

Brighdie, Milan, 1991

Jeanette Schaefers, Bucks County, Pennsylvania, 1985

These are what I call my
Calvin Klein shots.

Calvin was shooting men in his underwear but not women at the time. People seem to think that a photograph of a woman in underwear in this position should be censored, but New York is covered with similarly clad men in this same pose.

Why is it okay for·men but not for women?

I think it's fine for both. I see female photographers do pictures that I would never dare show, and they get encouragement. When a man does the same picture he's a chauvinist. There's such a double standard, especially when sexuality is the issue.

Kim Davis, Bucks County, Pennsylvania, 1985

Lea Sorenson, New York City, 1985

These pictures have been somewhat controversial. I'm not exactly sure why people see them as more provocative than other photos I've done.

Lea Sorenson, New York City, 1953

Cynthia and I did this whole series at a very small hotel in Paris called L'Hotel Montalambert, where a lot of fashion people used to stay. We were shooting for Italian *Vogue* in Place Pigalle, a place that has very risqué cabarets and sex stores and lots of hookers. Cynthia was intrigued by all the things in the sex stores, so we bought a few items, went back to the room, and did the shoot. I took the pictures with no equipment, no lights, nothing, except my camera and existing light.

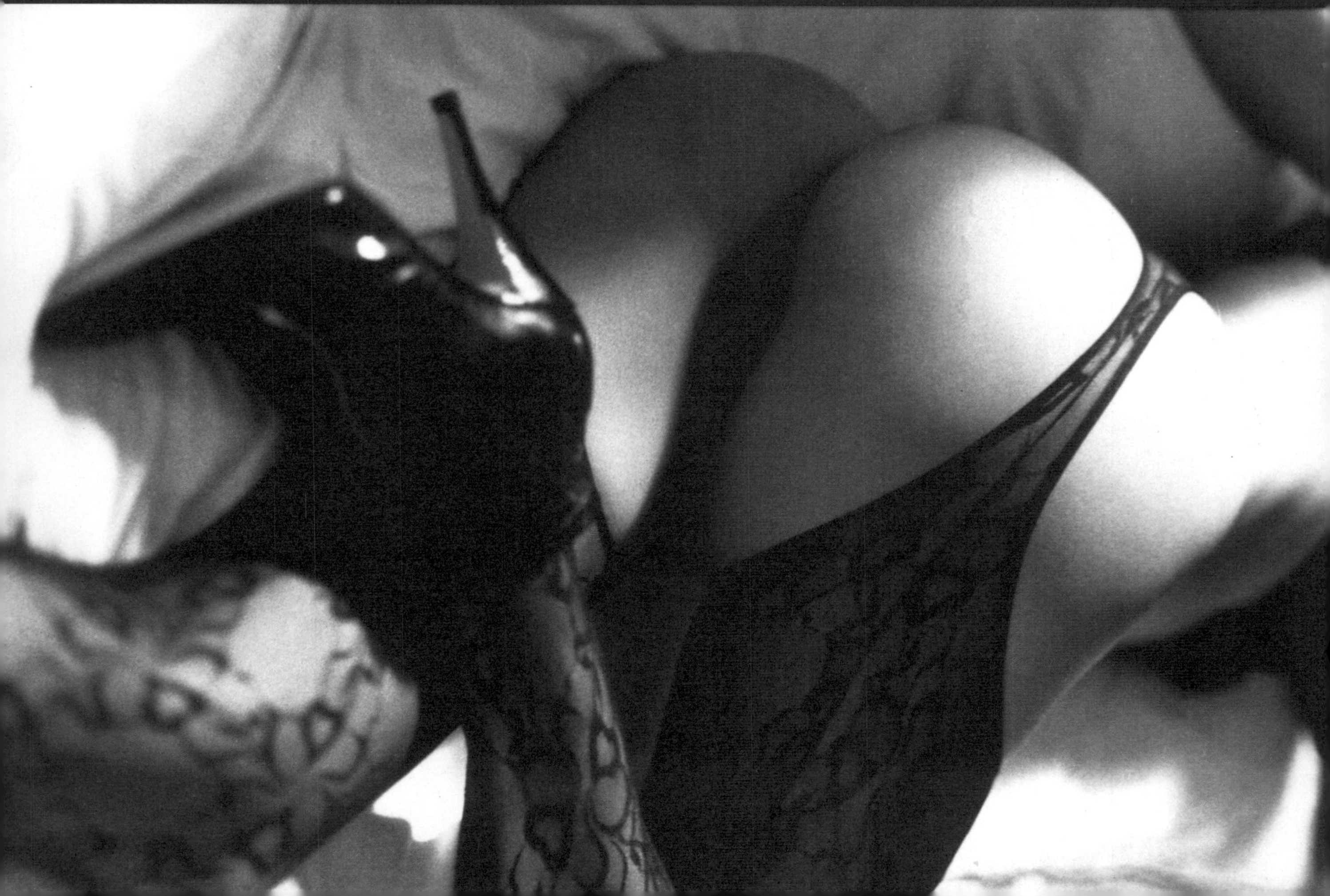

Cynthia Antonio, Paris, 1993

Cynthia Antonio, Paris, 1993

Daniela Pestova, St. Barth, 1993

*Many think
I'm tricking
everybody
into
exposing
themselves to
the world.
It's not like
that at all.*

THESE WOMEN WANT TO DO THESE PICTURES.

*I won't
shoot
with
someone
unless
they're
completely
comfortable
with it.
If the model
is tense
and nervous,
you just
won't get
good
pictures.*

Valerie Jean, New York City, 1996

Adriana Sklenarikova, New York City, 1996

Cecilia Nord, Milan, 1990

Carrie Nygren, New York City, 1990

I DON'T BELIEVE THAT WHAT I'M DOING IS IN
ANY WAY OFFENSIVE TO WOMEN AT ALL.
SEXUALITY IS NOT A VIOLENT OR BAD THING.
IT IS PART OF OUR VERY NATURE —
IT'S INNATE TO EVERY SINGLE HUMAN BEING.

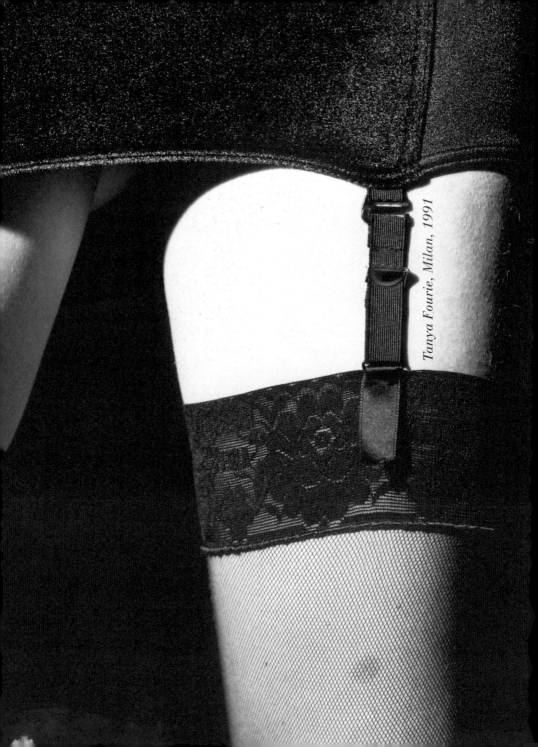

Tanya Fourie, Milan, 1991

BODY PARTS

Alexandra Brochen, Milan, 1991

Here's my

quintessential

fashion

photograph,

*and it could be
the best
fashion picture
I've ever taken.*

It's about

the dress,

not who's

wearing it.

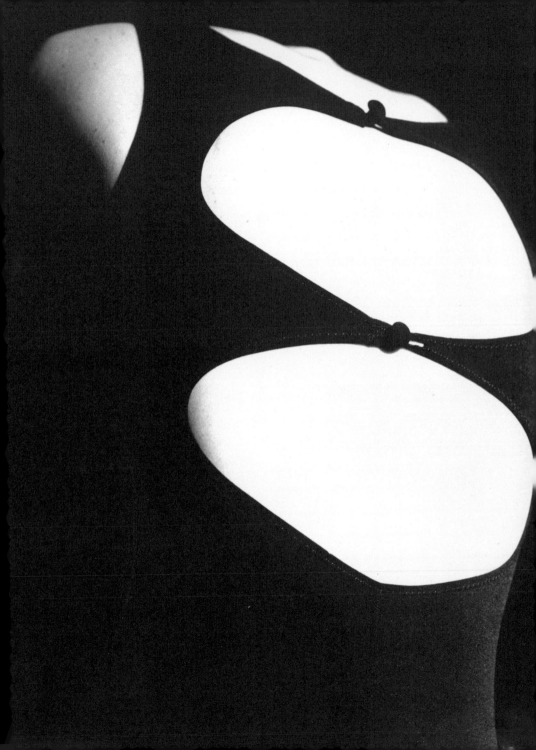

Alexandra Brochen, New York City, 1993

THE BODY BECOMES A LANDSCAPE.

You see valleys and hills,
plateaus and ravines,
gorges and sand dunes.
Ultimately,
I prefer the nude.
It's cleaner in
shape and line.

Suzanne Forbes, New York City, 1991

Alexandra Brochen, Milan, 19

Simona New York City 1994

Alexandra Brochen New York City 1993

Heidi, Milan, 1991

When I take pictures like these, I am looking at forms and thinking architecture and sculpture, light and shadows. I'm not very much attuned to the sexual component. A lot of people might not believe that, but it's true.

Suzanne Forbes, New York City, 1991

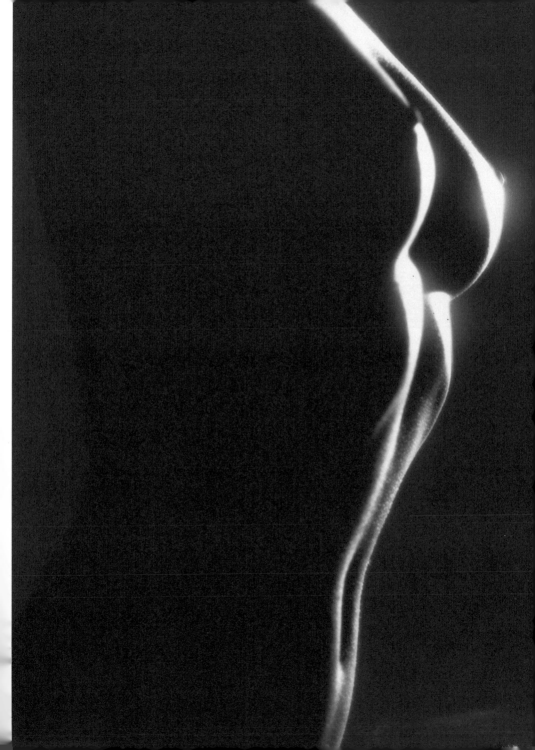

Alexandra Brochen

New York City 1993

Ingrid Seynhaeve, St. Barth, 1992

St. Barth, 1991

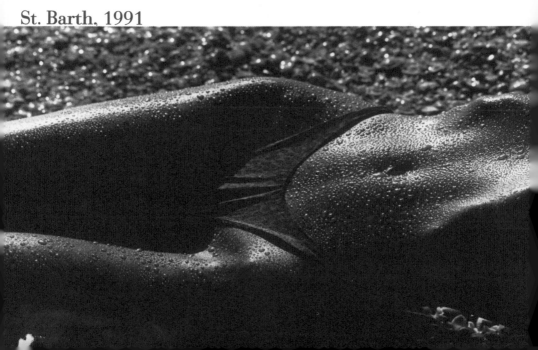

Ingrid Seynhaeve, St. Barth, 1992

UFO (Unidentified Fallen Object),
Lisa Ruthledge, St. Barth, 1984

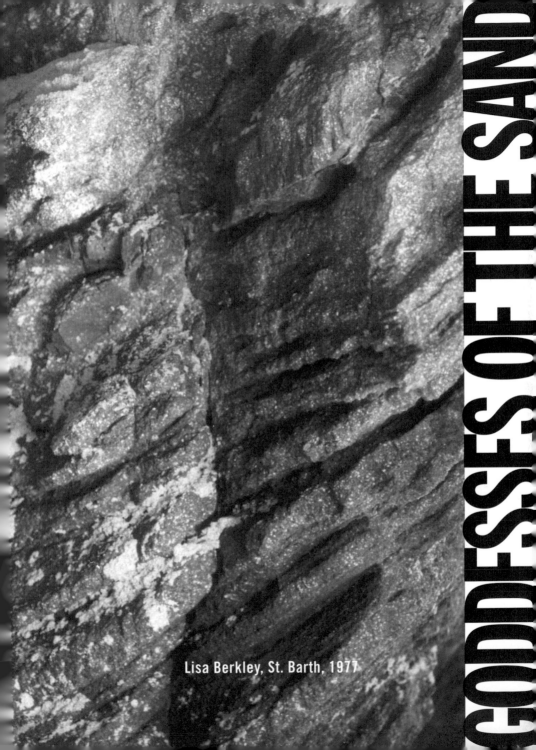

GODDESSES OF THE SAND

Lisa Berkley, St. Barth, 1977

Eva Herzigova, St. Barth, 1993

Cindy Crawford, St. Barth, 1989

ONE DAY I WAS IN ST. BARTH WITH M
SHE STARTED WASHING THE SAND OFF, BUT I SAID
IT OPENED A FLOODGATE OF SAND

Angie Everhart, St. Barth, 1990

Lisa Glaviano, St. Barth, 1989

WIFE TAKING PICTURES ON THE BEACH.
LEAVE IT THERE, AND LET'S SEE WHAT HAPPENS."
ND IT HASN'T STOPPED SINCE.

Amber Smith, St. Barth, 1993

Anna Falchi, Stromboli, 1995

Carrie Nygren, Monstique, 1986

I took the first woman-in-a-bathing-suit-with-sand shot back in 1976 or '77. Until then, everybody was painstakingly brushing every little grain of sand off the models' bodies. I remember it was one of the biggest jobs when shooting bathing suits; it was almost impossible to get all that sand off. We used to have assistants and editorial assistants with brushes and paper – anything that could be used to take all the sand away. This took forever, but nobody ever thought to leave it there.

Eva Herzigova, St. Barth, 1993

Elaine Irwin, St. Barth, 1989

Sophie Rousseau, St. Barth, 1993

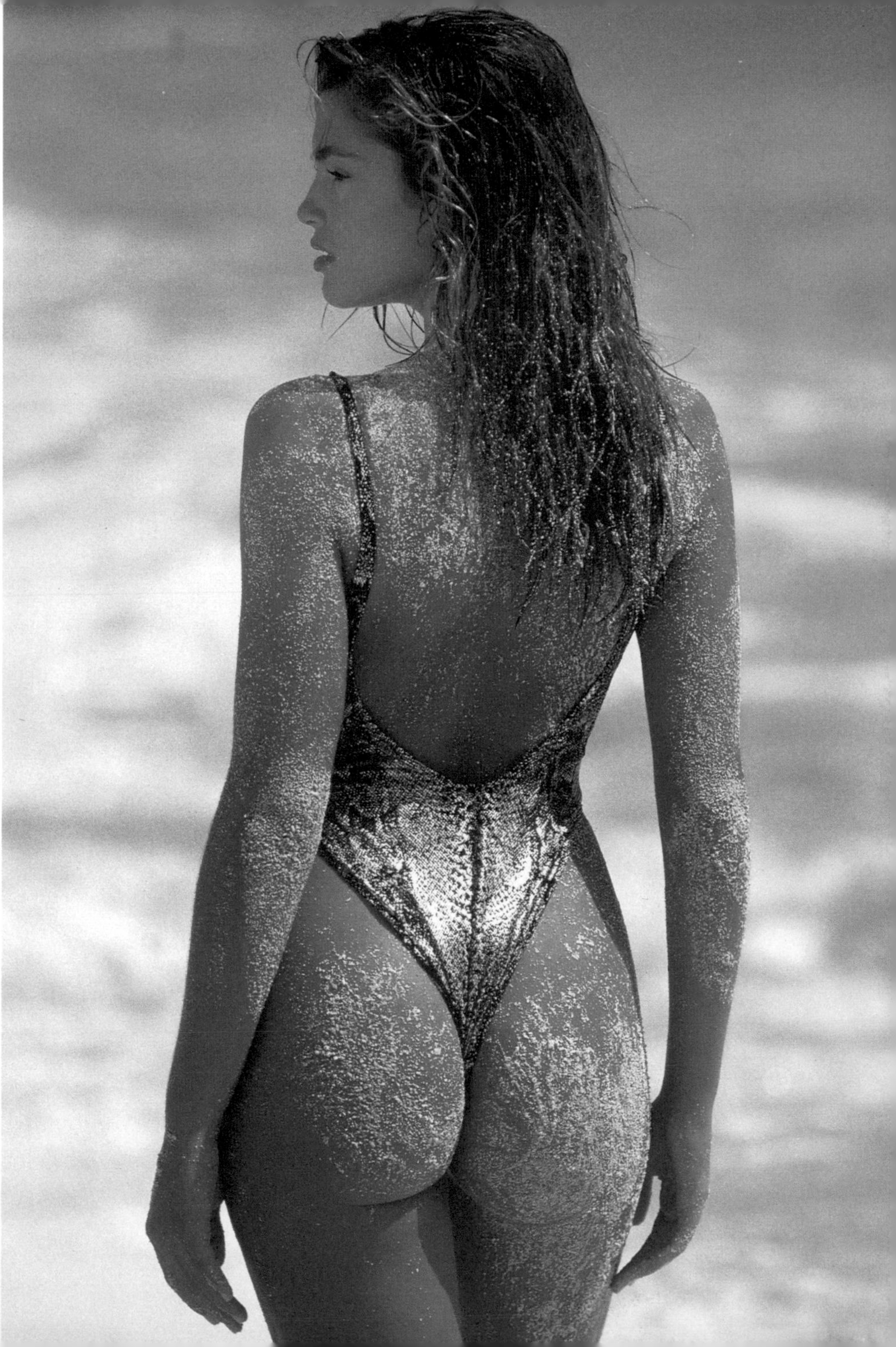

Cindy Crawford, St. Barth, 1989

*Tatjana Patitz
New York City, 1987*

Daniela Pestova, Bahamas, 1994

Eva Herzigova, St. Barth, 1993

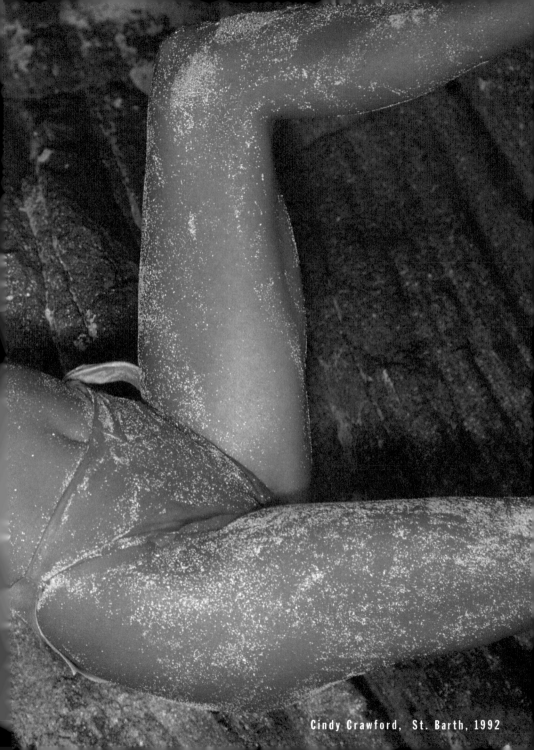

Cindy Crawford, St. Barth, 1992

"Naked Chicks on the Rocks"

*Anneliese calls all my pictures "Naked Chicks on the Rocks"
no matter what's in the photograph.*

The nice thing about Ashley is that she is such a large girl. I'm not saying fat, but very big. When you first look at her, it's hard to imagine her posing nude. Then, when she's in front of the camera, she completely transforms herself with movement.

It's amazing to see what she can do with her body.

Mel Flagler, St. Barth, 1992

Leslie Ann Woodward, St. Barth, 1994

Leslie Ann Woodward, St. Barth, 1994

I DON'T KNOW HOW IMPORTANT THE WOMEN REALLY ARE IN MY PHOTOGRAPHS. *Sometimes I wonder if I'm just doing landscape photography. I love a landscape with the human form in it. Maybe it's my architecture background. Rocks and water and trees with a woman – body, face, colors, texture – are beautiful together. It's not about a woman's soft body versus the roughness of nature, because* sometimes it's the nature that's soft, and the woman that's hard.

Angie Everhart, St. Barth, 1991

Amber Smith, St. Barth, 1992

I run into that scenario all the time: Husbands and boyfriends who don't want their wives or girlfriends to do pictures that the women are so eager to do. It doesn't make sense to me.

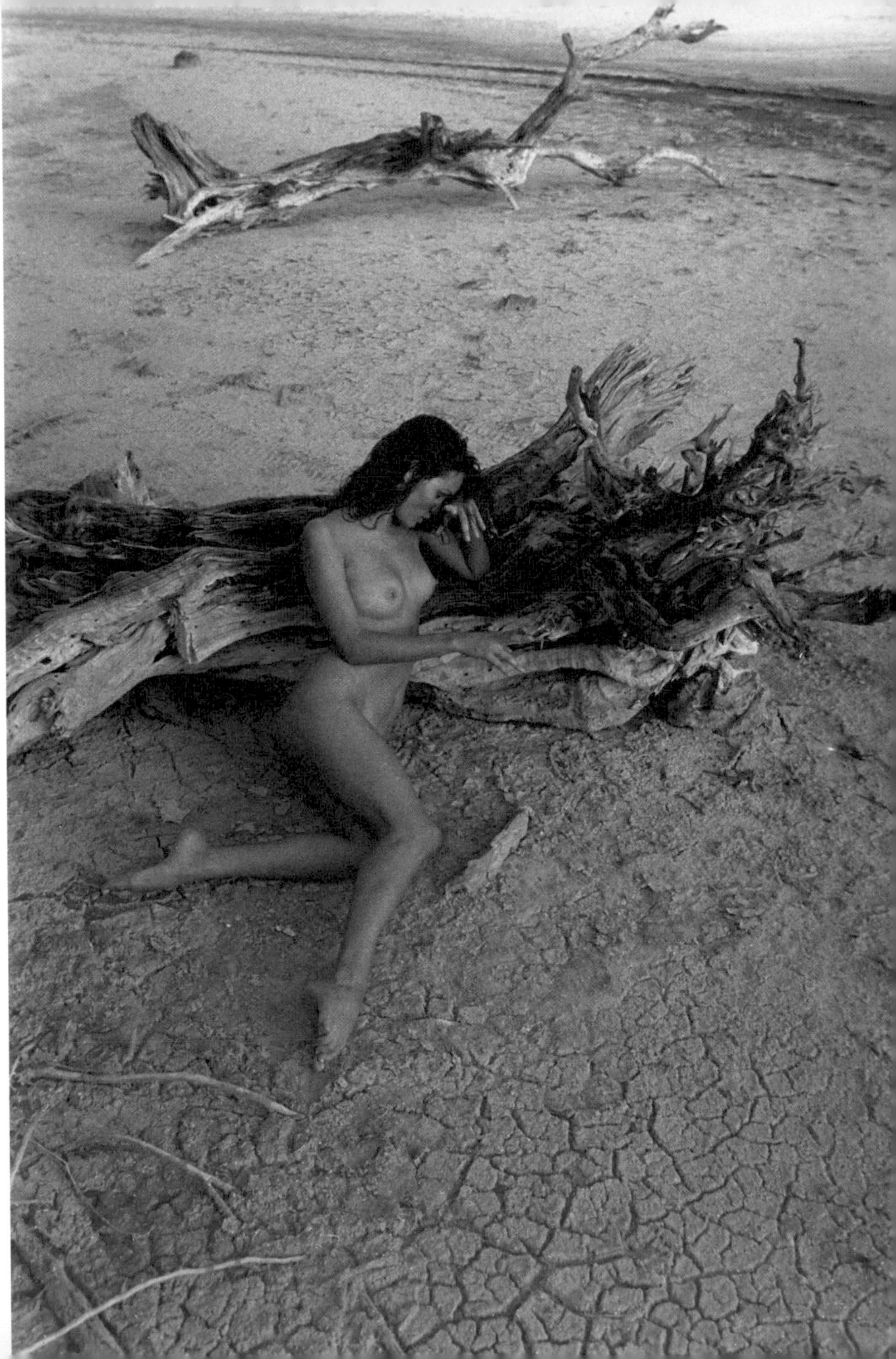

Mel Flagler, St. Barth, 1992

Cindy Crawford, St. Barth, 1989

KAIRLRISLESETNE N

Kirsten Allen, St. Barth, 1988

There was no shower at my studio, but, of course, we forgot about this little fact. It wasn't until after **Kirsten was completely covered in silver paint** that we realized she couldn't wash it off. In the same building on the sixth floor was a fencing academy where I was a member. Kirsten and I went down and showed up in the middle of all these fencers taking a class. The teacher was an old Hungarian in his late 70s, and I had to walk into the middle of his class with this naked woman covered in wet silver paint and say, "Excuse me, Master, may I use the shower?" I think they got a kick out of it.

Kirsten Allen, New York City, 1983

Kirsten Allen, Jamaica, 1989

Alexandra Brochen and Kirsten Allen, Jamaica, 1989

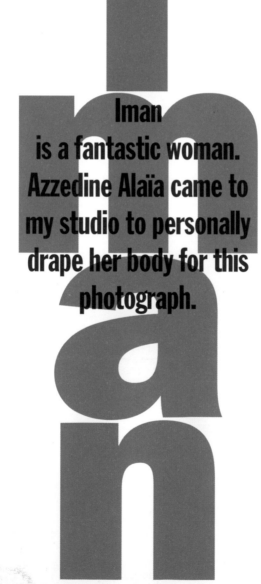

Iman
is a fantastic woman.
Azzedine Alaïa came to
my studio to personally
drape her body for this
photograph.

JOan Jseverance

"How did you talk Joan Severance into posing naked with a saxophone?"

I've been harassed many times about this picture. The truth of the matter is that Joan and I used to work a lot together, and we had a very good relationship. One day she called me and said, "I have a surprise. I want you to do this picture of me." When I met her at my studio, I found her naked in the dressing room with a saxophone. She said, "See, I'm learning the saxophone, and I want you to take a picture of me with it." Naturally, I was all for it.

Joan Severance, New York City, 1986

Ashley Richardson, Zuma Beach, California, 1988

Julie Anderson, Long Island, New York, 1989

Anna Nicole Smith

Before she became known, Anna Nicole was so shy. I was careful about her because I didn't want her to be offended by anything.

Anna Nicole Smith, Montclair, New Jersey, 1993

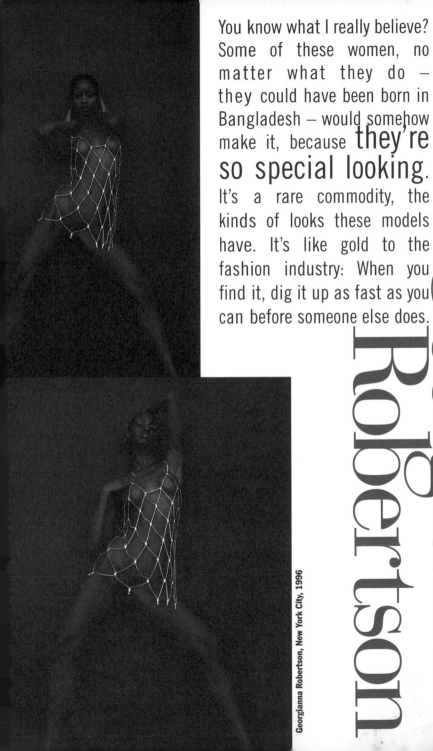

You know what I really believe? Some of these women, no matter what they do — they could have been born in Bangladesh — would somehow make it, because **they're so special looking.** It's a rare commodity, the kinds of looks these models have. It's like gold to the fashion industry: When you find it, dig it up as fast as you can before someone else does.

Georgianna Robertson

Georgianna Robertson, New York City, 1996

The best photos usually come in bunches. It has to do with how much energy I have, the day or the feeling, or the model and the place. It has to do with the chemistry between model and photographer, the crew, and the environment as well. Everyone has to be in sync at the same time, which doesn't really happen very often. There are so many people involved in shoots that one person just a little bit off or having a bad day can ruin the whole thing. Bottom line, it's all about good teamwork. The principal people are the photographer and the model, and it's crucial that they both feel very good about what's going on at the same time. There are many other variables: Boyfriends, girlfriends, wives, husbands, personal problems, missed connecting flights, location, weather, bugs, lost or damaged equipment, the time I broke my leg on a shoot – it's endless! So that rare day when everybody is relating and happy and wanting to do beautiful pictures makes it all worthwhile. Usually, on those days, I can get five or six good pictures. I might not get anything like that for another six months of shooting.

WOMAN ON A PEDESTAL

Some people may think

I'm just looking at women

as pretty objects.

That's not true.

I see my photographs

of them as objects,

but never the woman herself.

My photography is never accidental. I always have an idea for something before I shoot, and I often see the picture in my eyes, maybe the night before. Some images are more constructed than others, but there is always a clear concept first. Some people like the spontaneity of what happens when things are unplanned. I admire people who can do that, but it's not how I work.

Eva Malmström, New York City, 1978

Terry May, New York City, 1978

THIS WAS WHEN HI-TECH WAS REALLY BIG IN FASHION

AND DESIGN. THE IDEA I HAD WAS TO USE INDUSTRIAL MATERIALS INSTEAD OF CLOTHES, AND THIS IS HOW WE DRESSED THE GIRLS. IT DIDN'T WORK OUT TOO WELL. HOW MANY GOOD PICTURES CAN YOU MAKE WITH RUBBER BANDS AND MESH AND A NAKED WOMAN?

Behind the colored tubes was a white backdrop that masked a prop-storage space about four and a half feet wide. My martial arts teacher lived there for about a year.

Susan Jackson, New York City, 1979

Gunilla Bergstrom, New York City, 1978

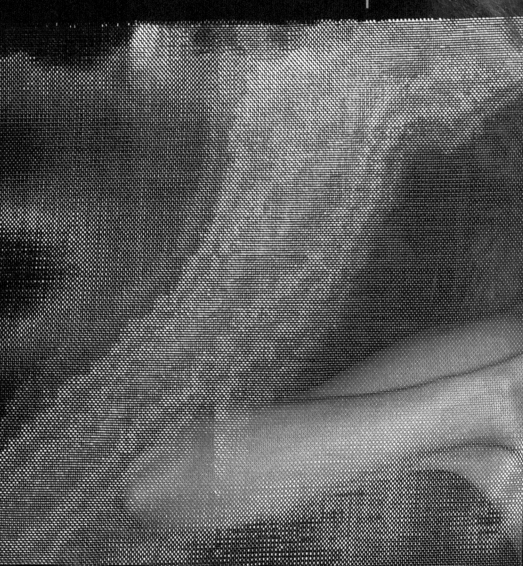

Carol Gramm, New York City, 1978

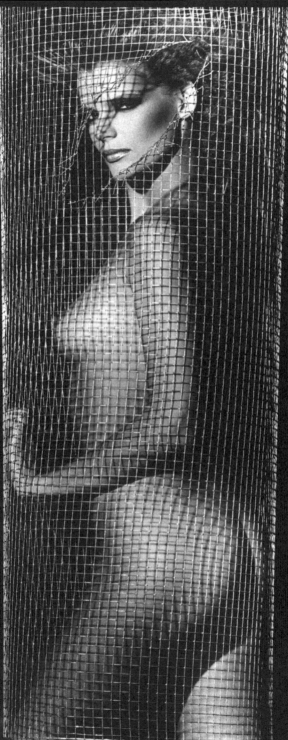

AMBER
SMITH

AMBER SMITH, ST. BARTH, 1992

AMBER SMITH, MILAN, 1991

Amber Smith, Milan, 1991

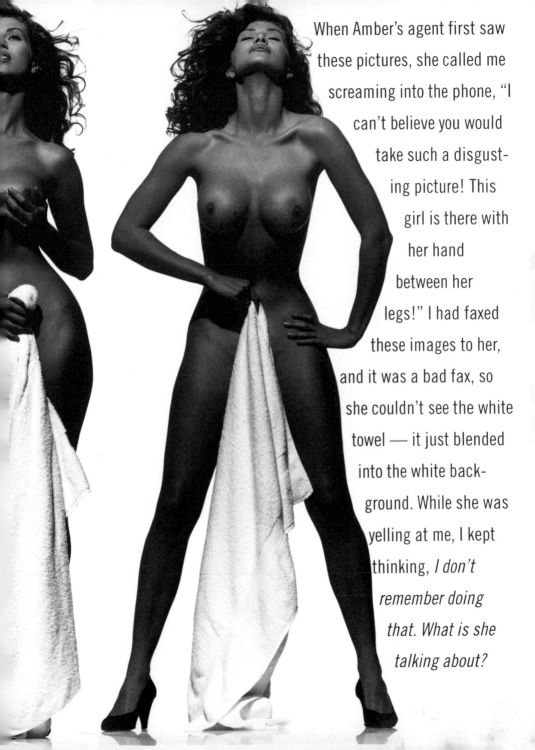

When Amber's agent first saw these pictures, she called me screaming into the phone, "I can't believe you would take such a disgusting picture! This girl is there with her hand between her legs!" I had faxed these images to her, and it was a bad fax, so she couldn't see the white towel — it just blended into the white background. While she was yelling at me, I kept thinking, *I don't remember doing that. What is she talking about?*

Dawn Heusser, Virgin Gorda, 1994

Anna Falchi, Stromboli, 1995

Lorena, Santorini, 1996

St. Barth, 1992

Ingrid Seynhaeve, St. Barth, 1992

Katja Halme, Santorini, 1996

John Casablancas sent me down to Jacksonville, Florida, to do a shoot with Kim Alexis. I decided to take Kristen, who was just starting out, along. We arrived at Kim's house,

When we got to this spot I asked, "What about the alligators?" Jimbo's reply was: "Don't worry, I've got a gun." After the shoot I took this picture of Kristen, who had to wear big swamp boots to protect her from the mud. Jimbo was standing by with his gun to shoot any alligators that might try to attack us. Somehow, in the middle of all this, Kristen managed to look totally relaxed.

but before we got to the house we passed all these warning signs: Trespassers Will Be Shot, Beware of Dangerous Dogs, and Trespassers Not Yet Eaten Will Be Shot.

We pulled up to the house, and we saw some very nasty-looking dogs locked in cages. Kim said the dogs were in cages because the alligators would eat them if they were loose. Kim's husband

at the time, Jimbo, led us all out to this wonderful semi-amphibious truck that drives over land and through water with no problem, and we headed out into the swamp.

ANNELIESE

I prefer very long, thi

very big breasts, I gues.

think they get in th

Tall, thin girls with dar

are very sexy to me

mistake of thinking tha

be my fantasy. S

women, and I don't like

because sometimes I

ay of elegance.

air and small breasts

eople often make the

hat I photograph must

ten that's not true!

Anneliese Seubert, Moustique, 1995

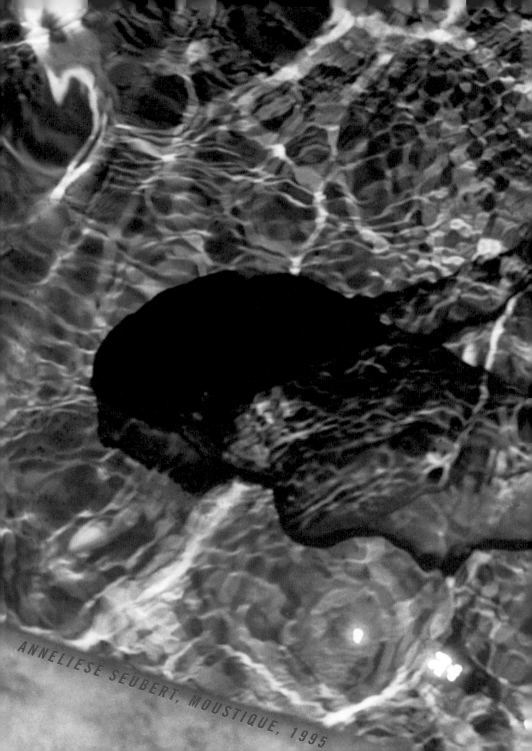

ANNELIESE SEUBERT, MOUSTIQUE, 1995

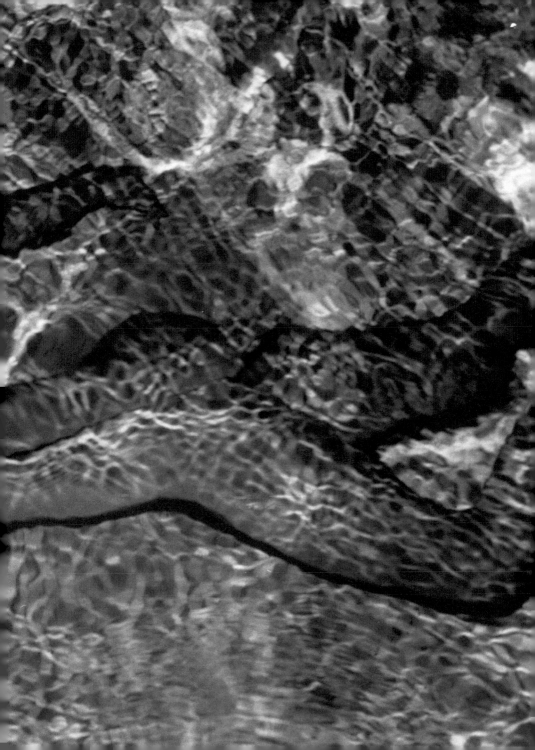

Color photography always leaves me a little cold, because it's too postcardy, too catalogue

Basia, Yuma, Arizona, 1994

There's much more room for interpretation and feeling and mood with black-and-white.

Anna Falchi, Stromboli, 1996

Aimee McKenney, Milan, 1996

MARIA GRAZIA CUCINOTTA

St. Barth, 1996

Maria Grazia Cucinotta, St. Barth, 1996

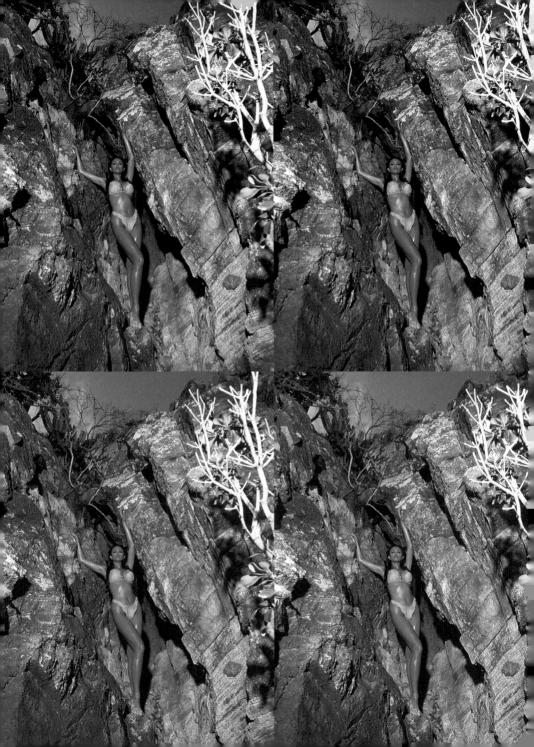

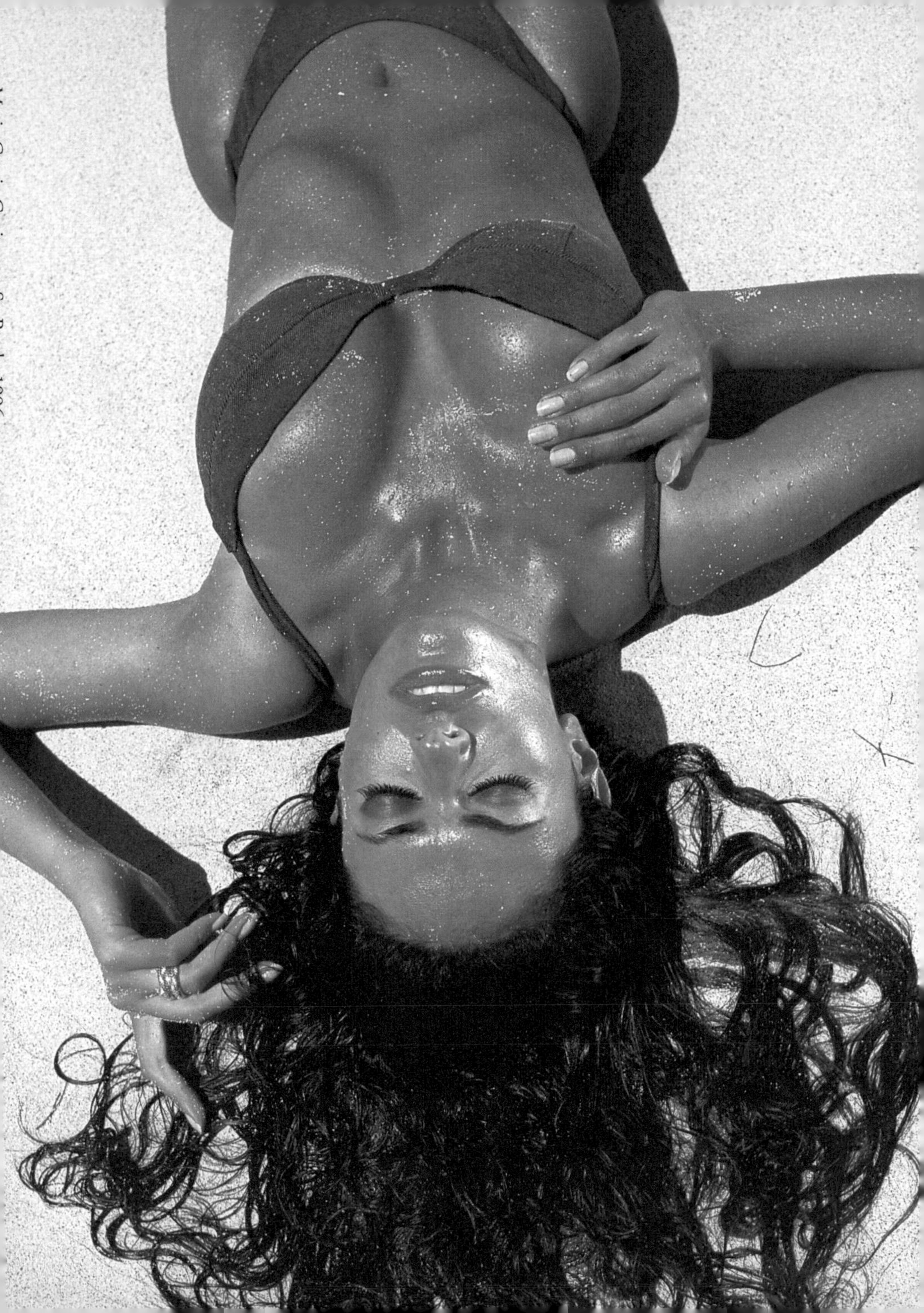

Maria Grazia Cucinotta St. Barth 1996

I'm not embarrassed to admit that I'm not interested in what's behind that veneer or what it means. When it comes right down to it,

I COULD MAKE A MURDERER LOOK LIKE AN ANGEL,

so it's not the inside that interests me. Don't get me wrong – photography is a very powerful tool to explore emotions, but that's not the way I'm using it. My aim is simply to preserve beautiful women.

Angie Everhart, Milan, 1989

BATHING
BEAUTIES

REBECCA ROM

SOUTH AFRICA, 1995

Alexandra Brochen, St. Barth, 1990

Cindy Crawford, St. Barth, 1989

On location for
Sports Illustrated

Editor Julie Campbell, Marco Glaviano, and the team, South Africa, 1995

Rebecca Romijn, South Africa, 1995

Cindy Crawford, St. Barth, 1989

Elizabeth, Moustique, 1987

Kirsten Allen, Moustique, 198

Eva Herzigova, St. Barth, 1993

Getting wet.

Alexandra Brochen, Jamaica, 1990

Gail Elliott, St. Barth, 1992

Paulina Porizkova, Anguilla, 1987
Daniela Pestova, Bahamas, 1994

Arlene Baxter, St. Barth, 1988
Paulina Porizkova, St. Barth, 1986

Eva Herzigova, St. Barth, 1992

Alexandra Brochen, St. Barth, 1990

I don't believe that the recipe for perfect happiness is through a beautiful body.

Elizabeth, St. Barth, 1990

Ingrid Seynhaeve, St. Barth, 199

Eva Herzigova
St. Barth
1993

Stephanie Seymour
New York City
1988

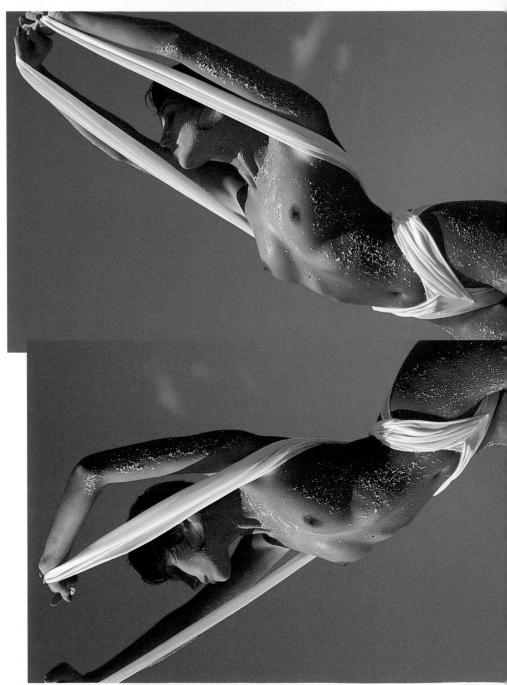

Elizabeth, Moustique, 1987

Some of my favorite pictures of all time are not nudes. Perhaps I've seen so many nude bodies, I'm immune to them now.

Angie Everhart, South Africa, 1995

I was born

in Sicily in 1942. In those days Sicily was somewhat backward in its ideas about society and what was considered acceptable behavior. It was, and still is in many ways, far behind the Western world – sort of stuck in an Italian version of the Victorian age. For one thing all schools were completely segregated by gender, and as a result I never laid eyes on a woman who wasn't my mother, a relative, or a nun until I was 15. There were strict rules about the kind of clothes you could wear in public. There was a judge

With my mother in Sicily, 1943

who used to throw the German tourists in jail, because they would come down on vacation wearing shorts. If you were caught by the police kissing a girl in a parked car, you'd get thrown in jail for that, too.

Fortunately, the arts flourished in this repressed atmosphere, and I was raised in a family for whom the arts were particularly important. One of my uncles was a

On location in Sardinia, 1969

prominent sculptor in Italy, and another uncle was a screenwriter, and our house was filled with paintings and sculpture, so I grew up surrounded by art and artists. The first nudes I ever saw (and for a long time the only nudes!) were in art. I remember a statuary in a Palermo fountain of 50 classical female nudes. I saw these naked women of white marble every day on my way to school,

On the way to visit my daughter Alessia, 1970

and I'm convinced it made a lasting impression. Even today there is a statuesque remoteness in my photographs that reminds me of those classical figures. When I was studying architecture at university, part of my visual training was to go around Palermo, full of centuries-old churches and hundreds of statues, and draw them. I guess this is where my appreciation

On location in Sudan, 1971

for classical forms of beauty comes from.

My mother was another strong influence. She used to let me watch her get ready for the theater, which was an elaborate affair in the '40s and '50s. She would spend two to three hours preparing: Applying makeup, fixing her hair, trying on gowns. And the hats she wore!

Playing with New Jazz Society, 1972

Her turbans were festooned with feathers and glittering with jewels. I remember thinking she was the most beautiful and elegant woman in the world, and I was completely entranced by the glamour of it all. My mother is probably the reason I got into fashion in the first place.

My screenwriter uncle gave me my first camera when I was five years old, but I didn't do much with it for a long time. My sister posed for me occasionally, but that was about it. By the time I was in university I was preoccupied with so many other things: I was playing vibraphone in a jazz group, studying for my architecture degree, plus designing

Fooling around in the studio with a championship bodybuilder, 1976

stage sets for the theater. I was taking pictures on the side

Photograph by Antonio Bellomo

In the studio with Niki Taylor, 1992

too, and developing the film in a makeshift darkroom in my closet. It got to the point where I didn't have time to do it all, so I chose to focus on photography. It was very simple: I enjoyed taking pictures of beautiful things, and it was a form of instant gratification for me. When my professor tried to convince me to continue with a career in architecture, I told him: "Look, if I do a bad building it's going to be there for years for all to see. One of the good things about photography is that if I do a bad photograph, it's not going to stick around for that long."

When I was 25, I left Sicily for Milan to seek my

Photograph by Lisa Glaviano

St. Barth, 1991

fortune as a fashion photographer. Since I had no formal training, I exaggerated my actual experience a bit to get that first assignment. The magazine was *Amica*, and they sent a big-name model to the rather bare studio I had set up in a small loft. I was so nervous, I remember thinking, "I hope she knows what to do, because I have no idea!" That was the beginning, and from there I just learned on the job.

I wasn't anyone's assistant so things moved quickly for me. In the late '60s there was such a feeling of camaraderie among people in the fashion industry in Milan. It was a

My daughter Alessia and sister Adriana, 199

small group of people, all starting out at the same time. We used to hang out at Bar Jamaica every night, helping one another and sharing ideas. Everyone was so naive and enthusiastic, because this was before fashion became

really big business. A group of extraordinary ladies at the fashion magazines then – most of them now editors-in-chief and creative directors – used to really help us out, too. I was very lucky to have been in Milan at that time.

With my daughter Barbara, 1996

    I didn't really start shooting nudes and women in bathing suits until I came to America in 1975. It was right around that time that I decided to do a book of nude women "dressed" in industrial materials. My mod-

With Monique Pillard, 1994

els for the project were the biggest in the industry, so they were completely comfortable with their bodies and very professional. I was well established in fashion by this time, so they were confident I'd take good pictures of them – they *wanted* to participate in the project! It hasn't stopped since.

The pictures in this book represent only a small percentage of the amount of work I've done over the past 25 years, but it happens to be my best-known work. Beautiful women are not the only subjects I photograph, but they are what the public wants to see. That's just the

In Sicily with my daughter Adrianna and Anneliese, 1995

way it is. The great thing is that so many of the pictures in this book have never before been published. I'm grate-ful for the opportunity.

New York City, July 10, 1996

Acknowledgments

I would like to extend a warm thanks to the following:

First and foremost, to all the models who have made this book possible, especially, to name just a few: Paulina, Cindy, Stephanie, Eva, Angie, and Anneliese for sharing so many days with me and my camera.

To Leonardo Mondadori and Nicholas Callaway for bringing this book to life, and to my editor, Andrea Danese, without whose dedication and commitment this book would not be here today. Also to Toshiya Masuda, whose graphic design greatly enhances sometimes less than perfect pictures, and to Lisa Glaviano for her help with editing the photographs.

To Anna, Lisa, Lisa, and Annalisa, who are forever part of my life, and to Eva M., whose best pictures are not in this book, because I never got her permission.

To my daughters Barbara, Alessia, and little Adrianna, who are so patient with their unconventional dad, and of course to my sister Adriana, my first model and the most beautiful of all.

To Daniela Giussani, Giovanna Mazzetti, Franca Sozzani, Michela Bardini, Milva Gigli, Carlo and Cristina Dansi, Julie Campbell, Monique Pillard, Federico Pignatelli, Nino Martire, Serge and Tatiana Sorokko, Bob and Winnie Uricola, Jean-Jacques Naudet, Rick Kantor, and Anne Price for funding and otherwise supporting so many of the pictures in this book.

To my friends and collaborators Antonio Bellomo, Suzanne Forbes, Camilla Olsson, Shannon Ornstein, Thad Quinlan, Jose Corredera, Maurizio Bacci, and Kris Kicior, and also to Tony Behar, Worth Poole Gurley, Vito Giangaspero, Mark Anthony Jorio, Katsuya Arai, Koji Masui, Hiromasa Sasaki, Paul Shimaura, and Wade Watson.

To Chuck Kelton for some of the best black-and-white prints, and Tonino Fodale for improving many of the prints.

I would like to extend a special thank you to the efforts of some of the best hair and makeup artists in the world, including: Richard Adams, Margaret Avery, Billy B., Michael Baker, Way Bandy, Renato Bernardi, John Birchall, Linda Cantello, John Caruso, Nando Chiesa, Giuseppe Ciulla, Gad Cohen, Dickey, Barbara Farman, Fulvia Farolfi, Pep Gay, Giorgio, Rodney Groves, Marie Laurie Gryson, Hamid, Ruby Hammer, Frances Hathaway, Susan Houser, François Ilnseher, Deborah Jean, Cindy Joseph, Sonia Kashuk, David Kiningson, Stephen Knoll, Hiromi Kobari, Mauritzio Kulpherk, Marie-Josee Lafontaine, James Le Bon, Stephane Lempire, Sophie Levy, Sandy Linter, Vincent Longo, Kevin Mancusa, Linda Mason, Maurizio Massari, Joe McDevitt, Sam McKnight, Patrick Melville, Ṣacha Mitic, Pier Giuseppe Moroni, Roberto Nardezzi, Andrea Paoletti, John Sahag, Carol Shaw, Carmon Springs, Mario Stagi, Ronnie Stam, Edward Tricomi, Robert Vano, Gabriele Vigorelli, Pru Walters, Michel Weeks, Scott Weinstein, Wendy Whitelaw, and Mauro Zorba.

Jill Goodacre, Haiti, 1984

A portion of the proceeds from this book will be donated to the Leukemia Society of America.

Sirens was produced by Callaway Editions, Inc., 70 Bedford Street, New York, NY 10014. Andrea Danese, editor. Toshiya Masuda, Esther Bridavsky, designers. Robert Janjigian, consulting editor. True Sims, Director of Production. Jessica Allan, Production Supervisor.

This book was designed on the Power Macintosh 9500 using QuarkXPress 3.3 and Adobe Illustrator 6.0 software. Typefaces include Bauer Bodoni, Bell Gothic, Deco, Didot, Franklin Gothic, Perpetua, STAPortable, Trade Gothic, and Triple Condensed Gothic.

This book was printed and bound by Palace Press International, Hong Kong.

FRONT COVER: Alexandra Brochen, St. Barth, 1990
BACK COVER: Anna Falchi, Stromboli, 1995

Cover design by Esther Bridavsky

PAGE 3: Eva Herzigova, St. Barth, 1993
PAGE 5: Julie Anderson, Long Island, New York, 1989
FRONTISPIECE: Eva Herzigova, New York City, 1994 (detail)

Warner Books, Inc.
1271 Avenue of the Americas
New York, NY 10020

Visit our Web site at http://pathfinder.com/twep

A Time Warner Company

Printed in Hong Kong

FIRST PRINTING: October 1997

10 9 8 7 6 5 4 3 2 1

ISBN: 0-446-91245-X

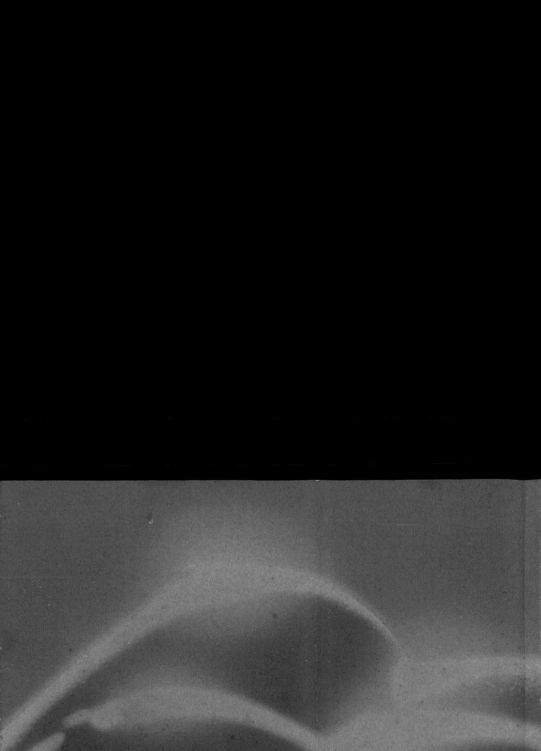